HAVE FUN READING THIS BOOK!

IT OFFERS SOME REAL **SURVIVAL TIPS.** BUT THE SETTINGS **ARE NOT REAL.** **THINK** ABOUT HOW YOU CAN USE THESE **HACKS** IN REAL LIFE. USE **COMMON SENSE.** **BE SAFE** AND **ASK** AN **ADULT** FOR **PERMISSION** AND **HELP** WHEN NEEDED.

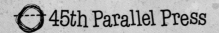
45th Parallel Press

Published in the United States of America by Cherry Lake Publishing
Ann Arbor, Michigan
www.cherrylakepublishing.com

Reading Adviser: Marla Conn, MS, Ed., Literacy specialist, Read-Ability, Inc.
Book Designer: Felicia Macheske

Photo Credits: © HN Works/Shutterstock.com, cover; © Dennis W Donohue/Shutterstock.com, 5; © Matt Jeppson/ Shutterstock.com, 6; © c12/Shutterstock.com, 9; © Potapov Alexander /Shutterstock.com, 11; © Mega Pixel/ Shutterstock.com, 11; © Africa Studio/Shutterstock.com, 13; By KKulikov/Shutterstock.com, 13; © Koldunov/ Shutterstock.com, 14; © Feng Yu/Shutterstock.com, 17; © Scisetti Alfio/Shutterstock.com, 19; © Aggie 11/ Shutterstock.com, 21; © koigeorgi/Shutterstock.com, 22; © kaushik.kashish/Shutterstock.com, 25; © spaxiax/ Shutterstock.com, 27; © Jacek Chabraszewski/Shutterstock.com, 29

Other Images Throughout: © SrsPvl Witch/Shutterstock.com; © Igor Vitkovskiy/Shutterstock.com; © FabrikaSimf/ Shutterstock.com; © bulbspark/Shutterstock.com; © donatas1205/Shutterstock.com; © NinaM/Shutterstock.com; © Picsfive/Shutterstock.com; © prapann/Shutterstock.com; © S_Kuzmin/Shutterstock.com © autsawin uttisin/ Shutterstock.com; © xpixel/Shutterstock.com; © OoddySmile/Shutterstock.com; © ilikestudio/Shutterstock.com; © Kues/Shutterstock.com; © ankomando/Shutterstock.com; © andromina/Shutterstock.com; © HN Works/ Shutterstock.com

45th Parallel Press is an imprint of Cherry Lake Publishing.

Library of Congress Cataloging-in-Publication Data

Names: Loh-Hagan, Virginia, author.
Title: Hunted by predators hacks / by Virginia Loh-Hagan.
Description: Ann Arbor, MI : Cherry Lake Publishing, [2019] | Series: Could you survive? | Includes bibliographical references and index.
Identifiers: LCCN 2019006165| ISBN 9781534147867 (hardcover) | ISBN 9781534150720 (pbk.) | ISBN 9781534149298 (pdf) | ISBN 9781534152151 (hosted ebook)
Subjects: LCSH: Survival—Juvenile literature. | Animal attacks—Juvenile literature. | Predatory animals—Juvenile literature.
Classification: LCC GF86 .L64255 2019 | DDC 613.6/9—dc23
LC record available at https://lccn.loc.gov/2019006165

Cherry Lake Publishing would like to acknowledge the work of The Partnership for 21st Century Skills. Please visit *www.p21.org* for more information.

Printed in the United States of America
Corporate Graphics

Dr. Virginia Loh-Hagan is an author, university professor, former classroom teacher, and curriculum designer. In the mornings, her dogs attack her to wake her up. Her dogs might be predators. She lives in San Diego with her very tall husband and very naughty dogs. To learn more about her, visit www.virginialoh.com.

COULD YOU SURVIVE

BEING HUNTED

BY PREDATORS?

THIS BOOK COULD SAVE YOUR LIFE!

Predators are hunters. They're **carnivores**. Carnivores eat meat. Some predators are **scavengers**. Scavengers eat **carcasses**. Carcasses are dead bodies. Predators hunt **prey**. Prey are the hunted. They're killed for food.

Predators hunt, catch, and kill their prey. They have skills that make them good hunters. Some predators can smell really well. They can sniff out prey. Some predators are fast runners. They chase their prey down. Some predators **stalk**. They watch. They follow. Then, they attack. Some predators **ambush**. Some predators hunt as a team.

TIP Stay away from places with wild animals.

Predators have weapons. These weapons help them kill and eat. Some predators may have sharp teeth. They may have sharp nails. They may have strong jaws. They may have poison.

Some predators attack humans. They're called man-eaters. There are different types of predators. Animals can be predators. Some predators are big. Examples are sharks, tigers, and bears. Some predators are small. Examples are snakes and mosquitoes. Some predators have magical powers. Examples are vampires, werewolves, and dragons. Some humans are predators.

But not all prey are helpless. Some prey have powers and skills. They know how to defend themselves. They know how to hide. They know how to trick predators.

◀ ∙∙∙ ○○

TIP Never feed animals that you don't know.

All living things need food. What if you were the food? What if predators were chasing you? Don't fear. You might be one of the lucky survivors. You have to be smart. First, learn more about predators. Know their weaknesses. Second, stay alive. Get out of the predators' way.

Most importantly, know how to survive. Keep this in mind:

- You can only live 3 minutes without air.

- You can only live 3 days without water.

- You can only live 3 weeks without food.

This book offers you survival **hacks**, or tricks. Always be prepared. Good luck to you.

TIP Stay with other people. Wild animals stay away from groups.

SCIENCE CONNECTION

Charles Darwin was a British scientist. He came up with the idea of natural selection. This is also known as "survival of the fittest." Humans and animals evolve over time. Evolve means to change. Both humans and animals have babies. They create new generations. Each generation has to deal with different challenges. They may have different resources. They may have fewer resources. They develop traits that help them survive. The survivors live. They have children. These children look a little different from their parents. But they also inherit traits from their parents. Inherit means to take on. The new generations adapt. Adapt means to change. New generations develop features to fit their environments. They pass on these features to their future children. Darwin called this process "descent with modification." Descent means to have future generations. Modification means a change. Today, scientists call this process "evolution."

CHAPTER 1

KEEP THE FIRES BURNING!

Oh no! Predators are on your trail. Make a fire. Fire keeps away predators. It also helps you. You need fire to cook. You need fire to stay warm.

TIP Wear gloves when making fires. Be safe around fires.

HACK

1. Make a fire pit. Add wood. Add **tinder** for starting the fire. Tinder includes leaves and small twigs.

2. Chew gum. Save the foil wrapper.

3. Cut the wrapper into a strip. Fold the strip in half. Cut in half. Cut at an angle.

4. Open and unfold the wrapper. It should look like 2 triangles on top of one another.

5. Attach the ends of the foil to the ends of a battery.

6. Watch the foil light on fire. Add the flame to the tinder in the fire pit.

TIP Use smoke to hide your smell from predators. Smoke also hurts eyes.

explained by
STEM

The key to this hack is the circuit.

Electric circuits are paths. Closed circuits form a loop. They're lines through which electricity flows.

In this hack, the joining of the foil creates a circuit. The foil connects the battery. Batteries have negative and positive ends. Charges flow from the negative end to the positive end. They do this quickly.

The thinness of the foil increases its **resistance**. Resistance is a force that drags. Foil isn't made to hold heat. So, heat has nowhere to go. It makes a flame. The flame has to be quickly transferred to tinder. Otherwise, it will die out.

CHAPTER 2

SEE AT NIGHT!

Many predators see very well. They can see from far away. They can tell how far away prey is. They can see how fast prey moves. Some predators are **nocturnal**. Nocturnal means active at night. Get night vision so you can see at night.

HACK

1. Get a flashlight. Flashlights are tools. They shine light on things.

2. Get red nail polish. (Use red plastic wrap if you don't have polish.)

3. Paint over the lens. Paint a couple of layers.

4. Test the light. Make sure there aren't any leaks of white light. If so, paint on more red.

TIP Go for the eyes.
This is a self-defense move.

explained by STEM

The key to this hack is light.

Color travels in waves. Some colors are easier to see than others. Light helps us see color.

White light is bright. It's a mix of all colors. Humans can see things lit by white light. The sun and lamps make white light. White things reflect back all the color waves. Colored things reflect back some of the waves. They absorb the other waves.

Humans have a hard time seeing at night. Human eyes need time to get used to darkness. Bright light doesn't let humans see in the dark. Red light doesn't look as bright to human eyes. It has the least effect on night vision.

TIP Shine red light. Red can also mean emergency.

REAL-LIFE CONNECTION

Beagles are dogs. They're small hounds. Hounds are hunting dogs. There are hunting beagle contests. Beagles hunt rabbits. But they don't kill rabbits. They get points for finding rabbits. They get points for circling rabbits. They have to do this in about 2 hours. About 500 dogs compete. Halfway Annie B is a beagle. She's a world champion. She won in 2010. She was the youngest dog to win. She was 16 months and 4 days old. Her owner described her as "a very consistent dog that will jump plenty of rabbits and turn on a dime when they're up and running." Annie became famous. She was on the cover of magazines. She's very loved. But she wasn't always loved. When she was born, she was the dog that nobody wanted. She was the last in her litter. Litters are groups of young animals. They're born at the same time.

CHAPTER 3

HIDE IN NATURE!

Stay away from predators through **camouflage**. Camouflage means blending in. It means disguising. Hide your smell. Hide your looks. Make natural paints.

TIP Use a tree brush.
Brush out your tracks as you move.

HACK

1. Get things that have different colors. Examples are berries and green plants.

2. Mash these things up in a bowl. Use a fork. (To make green, boil the plants. Use the green water.)

3. Use a strainer. Collect the juice. Put the juice in a container.

4. Add some eggs or honey. (If you have flour, use that.) This thickens the mixture into a natural paint.

5. Get plants that have a smell. Examples are mint and lavender. Rub them. Add to the paint. This hides your smell.

6. Add water and spit. Mix.

7. Spread all over your body.

STEM

The key to this hack is **chemistry**.

Chemistry is a science. It's the things that make up substances. As substances mix, they change. They turn into something else.

Paint is made of **pigments**, **binders**, and **solvents**. Pigments are colors. They can come from nature, minerals, or oil. In this hack, the berries and plants provide the pigments.

Binders join things together. They make pigments stick. They make paint stick to your skin. They keep paint on after it dries. In this hack, binders are spit, eggs, and honey.

Solvents dissolve substances. Dissolve means to melt into something. They make paints thin or thick. In this hack, water is the solvent.

TIP Use mud as camouflage.

CHAPTER 4

MAKE SOME NOISE!

Most predators have good hearing. Make sounds. Distract predators away from you. Use sound to scare animals away. Make **wind chimes**. Wind chimes make tinkling sounds.

TIP Stay still. Predators can hear prey move.

HACK

1. Get some wood sticks of different sizes. Scrape the bark off. (Bamboo makes the loudest sound.)

2. Get things that make sound. Examples from nature are pinecones and hard shells. Other examples are tin cans and spoons.

3. Get long leaves. Rip into strips. Braid together. Make into a circle.

4. Get string. Tie the items to the circle. Space them so there's enough room to clink against each other.

5. Tie an object in the center.

6. Tie string to the circle. Use this as the hanger.

7. Tie wind chimes to a tree branch. Make more wind chimes. Place them on different branches.

explained by STEM

The key to this hack is the wind.

Wind is moving air. It's caused by differences in air pressure. Air in high pressure moves to areas in low pressure. The greater the difference in pressure, the faster the air flows.

Wind makes wind chimes move. When the objects move, they bump into each other. They also bump into the center object. The center object is called the **clapper**. This bumping makes **vibrations**. Vibrations are sound waves. The waves travel down the objects. They make different sounds. The sounds depend on the length and material. Big, long tubes make low, deep sounds. Short, thin tubes make high sounds.

TIP Make loud noises. This can be a call for help.

SPOTLIGHT BIOGRAPHY

Michelle Jewell is a scientist. She studies animal behaviors. She mainly studies predators and prey. She studies animals in different places. She's been to Antarctica. She's been to jungles. She's been to oceans. She went to Florida. She studied sea turtles. She saw a half-eaten sea turtle. She wasn't grossed out. She was fascinated. She said, "This was a massive female sea turtle sliced in half by the teeth of (presumably) a tiger shark. And, in that moment, I realized I was to study those things! ... I've always loved predators, from red-tailed hawks in my backyard to jellyfish gobbling up zooplankton and white sharks chasing seals." She calls herself a "shark scientist." She goes where sharks go. But she stays hidden. She wants to observe sharks. She doesn't want to interfere. She thinks sharks should be sharks. She's one of the few female shark scientists. She encourages more girls to study sharks.

CHAPTER 5

TRAP A BEAST!

Make traps. This hack is called the Greasy String **Deadfall**. Greasy means oily. Deadfalls are traps that use a heavy object.

TIP Learn what predators like to eat.

HACK

1. Get something to act as a deadfall. Examples are flat rocks or heavy logs.

2. Get a **forked** stick. Forked means being V-shaped.

3. Get a **stake**. Stakes are pointed posts.

4. Get string. Or use **saplings**. Saplings are young trees.

5. Tie the string to one fork of the stick. Tie the other end to the stake.

6. Drive the stake into the ground.

7. Cover the string in **bait**. Bait is something predators eat. This could be meat.

8. Raise up the deadfall object. Put it on the string. Put it between the stick and stake.

explained by STEM

The key to this hack is gravity.

Gravity is a force. It attracts things to the Earth's center.

Predators are lured to the trap. They eat the bait. They lick the string. The string could snap. Or the **trigger** stick is pushed away. Triggers are tools that set things loose. Either way, the deadfall falls. It'll land on top of the predator. This could kill or harm the predator.

The deadfall falls because of gravity. **Impact** force is created. Impact means a crash. Impact force happens when 2 things crash. It delivers shock as energy. Energy moves from the deadfall to the predator.

TIP Run and hide. Traps give you time to do this.

DID YOU KNOW?

- Humans fear sharks. But sharks kill fewer than 10 people each year. Snakes kill around 50,000 people each year. Humans kill the most. They kill about 475,000 other people each year. This mainly happens because of wars.

- Tigers are predators. They've killed more people than any other big cat. The Champawat Tiger was a female Bengal tiger. She killed over 430 people in Nepal and India. She's in the *Guinness Book of World Records*. An army tried to hunt the tiger. It failed. Jim Corbett was a British hunter. He shot the tiger in 1907.

- Of all predators that have attacked humans, wolves have the lowest number of human deaths. The majority of wolf kills have been children. Wolves live close to cities. This means they're not scared of humans. Humans have tried to feed wolves. This is not a good idea. Wolves are not dogs.

- A skull of an African boy was found. It was found in Taung, South Africa. The boy was only 3 years old. He lived millions of years ago. His skull had holes in the eye area. Scientists think a large bird grabbed the boy. The bird carried the boy in the air. Then, it dropped him in its nest. The bird was related to an African crowned eagle.

- The biggest predator is tiny. Mosquitoes are bugs. They've killed billions of humans. They carry diseases. They bite humans. They make humans sick. These sicknesses can lead to death. Mosquito bites kill over 700,000 people each year.

- Piranha are fish. They have teeth. One piranha is not very scary. But a group of piranha is a different story. A shoal is a large number of fish swimming together. A shoal of piranha overwhelm their prey. They've been known to take down prey the size of humans.

CONSIDER THIS!

TAKE A POSITION!

Predators sound scary. But they're a necessary part of the food chain. We need predators. Learn more about predators. Explain how predators are helpful. Explain how they're harmful. Are predators more helpful or harmful? Argue your point with reasons and evidence.

SAY WHAT?

All predators have prey. All predators have predators. Pick an animal. Explain the animal's position in a food chain. List the animal's predators. List the animal's prey.

THINK ABOUT IT!

If you could be any predator, which predator would you be? Why? Learn more about this predator. What strengths would you have? What weaknesses would you have?

LEARN MORE!

Claybourne, Anna, and David Burnie (illust.). *Scanorama: Deadly Predators*. San Diego, CA: Silver Dolphin Books, 2016.

Loh-Hagan, Virginia. *Top Ten: Predators*. Ann Arbor, MI: Cherry Lake Publishing, 2016.

Wilsdon, Christina. *Ultimate Predatorpedia: The Most Complete Predator Reference Ever*. Washington, DC: National Geographic Kids, 2018.

GLOSSARY

ambush (AM-bush) to attack by surprise

bait (BAYT) food used to lure animals as prey

binders (BINE-durz) things that bind or join things together

camouflage (KAM-uh-flahzh) blending into or hiding in the environment

carcasses (KAR-kuhs-iz) dead bodies

carnivores (KAHR-nuh-vorz) predators that eat meat

chemistry (KEM-ih-stree) the science of the composition, structure, and properties of substances and the changes they undergo

circuit (SUR-kit) a path between two or more points along which an electrical current can be carried

clapper (KLAP-ur) the object in the middle of wind chimes

deadfall (DED-fawl) a trap that uses a heavy object

forked (FORKD) having a V-shape

gravity (GRAV-ih-tee) force that attracts things to the center of the Earth

hacks (HAKS) tricks

impact (IM-pakt) a crash

nocturnal (nahk-TUR-nuhl) being active at night

pigments (PIG-muhnts) colors

predators (PRED-uh-turz) hunters

prey (PRAY) animals that are hunted and killed for food

resistance (rih-ZIS-tuhns) the force that drags or slows things down

saplings (SAP-lingz) young slender trees

scavengers (SKAV-uhnj-urz) predators that eat carcasses

solvents (SAHL-vuhnts) things that are able to dissolve other substances

stake (STAYK) a pointed post

stalk (STAWK) to watch and follow prey in order to hunt them

tinder (TIN-dur) things used to start a fire, like leaves and small twigs

trigger (TRIG-ur) a tool that sets something off

vibrations (vye-BRAY-shuhnz) waves that move up and down

wind chimes (WIND-chimez) clusters of small pieces that hang together and make tinkling sounds as they move in the wind

INDEX